'So, how doe i feel to have one's dream come true?' said the girl.

'What?' Sukey stood in the light little room feeling big and dirty.

'You're nine day, aren't you? Didn't you see your card?'

'My card.

'And you were, weren't you, just thinking how you'd like a sister? Perhaps gazing into the distance longingly? Imagining what she might look like?'

'A sis . . . ?' Sukey choked. 'I did, I think I did, yes, sort of mention a sister,' she admitted. 'Just to myself, just a thought . . .'

'Well, here I am!' she cried. 'Your twin sister.'

FINDERS, KEEPERS

Rebecca Lisle
Illustrated by the author

YEARLING BOOKS

FINDERS, KEEPERS

A YEARLING BOOK : 0 440 86337 6

First publication in Great Britain

PRINTING HISTORY
Yearling edition published 1995

Set in Monotype New Century Schoolbook by
Phoenix Typesetting, Ilkley, West Yorkshire.

Yearling Books are published by Transworld Publishers Ltd,
61–63 Uxbridge Road, Ealing, London W5 5SA,
in Australia by Transworld Publishers (Australia) Pty Ltd,
15–25 Helles Avenue, Moorebank, NSW 2170,
and in New Zealand by Transworld Publishers (NZ) Ltd,
3 William Pickering Drive, Albany, Auckland.

Made and printed in Great Britain by
Cox and Wyman, Reading, Berks.

For my real sister, Susanna

1. The Spangler Family

Sukey Spangler had twelve brothers.

This is no joke at any time, but on birthdays it's especially trying.

And today was Sukey's ninth birthday.

Her eldest brother, Ralph, was watching her as she unwrapped his gift. 'I do like useful presents,' he said.

'So I see,' said Sukey, turning the bottle-opener round in her fingers. 'That'll be really useful . . . when I'm eighteen.'

She put it down beside her other gifts: a bicycle pump and bicycle bell, torch, hamster wheel, packet of Smarties, woolly vest, miniature spanner, football jumper, book for

recording golf scores, and two packets
of caps for a gun.

'They're all lovely,' she said.

'Glad I didn't have to buy a Wendy
doll,' said Henry.

'Or a Sindy house,' said Elvis.

'You mean Sindy dolls and Wendy
houses,' said Sukey.

'Yah! Silly girlie stuff!' said Rikki.
'Who'd want it?'

Sukey sighed. 'Only some girlie person,' she said.

'You do like the hamster wheel?' asked Elvis. 'Mum said to get you something I'd like myself.'

'Yes, it's lovely.'

'Bit small for your rat, though.'

'Oh, Smelly won't mind and I haven't got a hamster at the moment,' said Sukey.

'Er, no . . . Er, funny, 'cos at the moment I have.'

Sukey handed the hamster wheel back to Elvis.

Billy borrowed back the bicycle pump he'd given her and took the bell too since Sukey didn't have a working bike just then.

The twins, John and Grant, came to show her their guns.

'Very smart,' said Sukey.

'Yeah, a sheriff's gun, actually. Shame we don't have any caps.'

'Caps are expensive,' said Grant.

'We've spent all our money on your

present so we can't buy caps but it doesn't matter or anything.'

Sukey handed over the two boxes of caps.

'It's all right,' said Danny, who'd been watching. 'I don't want to borrow my spanner back.'

Sukey looked at the tiny spanner. It was dented and rusty.

'I'm not surprised,' she said.

'I may be only five,' said Danny, 'but I know things.'

'Uh huh,' said Sukey.

'And I know that's a very special

...I know things

spanner. It may not be just exactly what you want this minute, but the minute *will* come when it's exactly what you want. You'll see.'

'Thank you,' said Sukey. 'You mean, perhaps, when I'm building a miniature bridge or model of the Eiffel Tower?'

'You never know,' said Danny, smiling as he wandered away.

Sukey quickly pulled on the woolly vest and the football jumper and was just eating the last Smartie when her father came in. His sleeves were rolled up and his hands were dirty with grease and dust.

'Darling! Having a brilliant birthday? That's a splendid new torch, think I might just borrow it? . . . I'm trying to finish the extension before the baby . . .'

'How is Mummy?'

Her father's worried expression caused a chill squeeze somewhere deep in Sukey's insides. 'Is she all right?'

'She's fine. Don't look so worried. I phoned the hospital earlier and they're both fine. It'll be all right,' he promised. 'These babies, well, they're strong little things.'

'I wish she were here. Mum, I mean.'

'I know, and the baby. Perhaps it'll come today, on your birthday!'

'I hope not, that would be awful!' cried Sukey. 'Oh, I wouldn't mind really, since it's late anyway,' she added, not wanting to sound mean. 'It can come any time just as long as it's all right!'

Once, ages and ages ago, one of the Spangler babies had died. Sukey hardly knew anything about it, not even its name, but she could picture it clearly, almost as if she had seen it once, and she knew it was sweet with smooth milky cheeks and a waxy glow on its skin, like an old doll. She could cry, quite easily, whenever she thought about it.

It was horrid not having her

mother here for this special day, but it was even worse thinking something might be wrong with the new baby or with Mum . . . And what if this one was the longed-for girl? A sister? But of course it wouldn't be, Sukey told herself. Girls just weren't what her parents made — except by mistake, like her.

2. The Birthday Tea-Party

Usually, the best thing about a Spangler birthday was the birthday cake. Mrs Spangler was the best birthday cake-maker for miles

around; she got so much practice. But this time the cake was from a shop, though it did have something sticky on top which was her father's home-made icing.

Everyone gathered around the massive table for tea. The boys were shouting and laughing but Sukey wasn't. Nothing about this birthday seemed quite right to her.

I wanted Cinderella plates, she thought, squidging the edge of her Star Trek one, and not leftover

Elvis Henry Rikki Ralph

John Grant

dinosaur dishes and spacemen cups. Even the cherryade tasted like the horrid pink drink at the dentist's. Nothing was right.

But nobody else seemed to think so. They were having lots of fun.

'I missed the match,' cried Rikki. 'Who won?'

'It was three-one, United,' said Sukey quietly.

'THREE-ONE, UNITED!' Claude shouted from several seats away.

'That means United got three goals and the other side only got one,' Rikki kindly explained to his sister.

Sukey made a sort of 'humph' sound, but no-one took any notice. The shouts and merry chatter went on around her.

'Carburettor's done for!'

'. . . spark-plugs . . .'

'. . . sprockets . . .'

'Donna, donna, donna, donna, BATMAN!'

'. . . Ferrari . . . blah, blah . . . Porsche . . .'

'Jingle bells, Batman smells, Robin flew away, Mr Silly lost his . . .'

'GRANT! Be quiet!'

Sukey listened and watched as if from a great distance.

Little Max was bouncing on her father's knee – soon he wouldn't be the baby any more. Who would replace him? What would they call it? Why didn't the phone ring right now and tell them the baby had come? It was two weeks late . . . Two whole weeks . . .

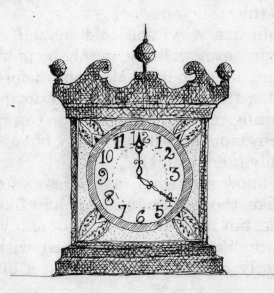

Sukey looked at the clock. Exactly four o'clock. The tea would go on for ages and the boys had probably forgotten who the party was for anyway. Nobody even notices me, she thought, nobody cares about me at all, and as if to test them she slipped off her chair and crept away to her room.

If only I had a sister, she thought for the hundredth, millionth time. If only, if only, if only . . . then I'd have someone who'd understand. It's not fair having only boys. Boys are so boyish!

But it's silly, she told herself. I mustn't ever wish the new baby to be a girl. I did it with Max and before that with Larry and it was so disappointing . . . No, there wouldn't ever be any more girls in the family, but oh, if only there could be!

I know just what my sister would be like, thought Sukey. Long hair like mine, but not quite as thick or shiny; a face like mine but perhaps with slightly big ears or something a bit

wonky so as not to be too pretty. She'll be much younger than me so I'll help her with everything and protect her. She could picture it exactly.

She took her pet rat, Smelly, from his box. He was good to cuddle and a patient listener. 'But the new baby's a boy,' she told Smelly sternly, 'and when he comes, it won't matter, because we'll all love him, won't we? I love you, don't I?'

She climbed on to the old toy box beneath the window and gazed out across the garden to where she imagined the hospital was. Hurry home, Mum, she urged.

Suddenly she stiffened. 'Yikes! Look, Smelly!'

There was a house or a shed – a building – just visible through the greenery at the end of the garden. There had certainly *never* been anything there before.

'How did that get there?' she asked Smelly. 'Perhaps it grew, like a mushroom? How odd! Come on, let's investigate!'

She stuffed Smelly inside her shirt, pulled on her baseball cap and set off.

Crossing the grass she had an odd sensation, as if she was stepping through a cold pocket of air or a chill current of water in the sea, and she shivered, almost turning back home, but then it passed, and the enticing red roof of the strange new house drew her on.

Nobody even noticed she had gone.

3. The Other Girl

The house was tiny, too small for a grown-up but just right for a Sukey-sized person. It made her think of the Seven Dwarfs' house, it was so pretty and small, like something from a fairy tale.

The door was open, so Sukey peeped in.

There were lace curtains and pink walls. Pictures of baby animals and shelves of cuddly toys. Two blue-eyed, blond dolls stared at her from the bed. It was very clean and tidy, and there were no bikes, no guitars or footballs to be seen.

Just the house I would have picked for myself, Sukey thought dreamily. Lovely!

There was a card on the table:

HAPPY BIRTHDAY! 9 TODAY!

That's odd, she thought, the person who lives here must be nine today, too!

Then suddenly she heard the noise of a motor and, going outside, saw a small pink car driving up to the house. It was a miniature car just right for a nine-year-old.

Sukey stared. The car was very odd but, even odder, the person driving it was . . .

HER . . !

SUKEY!

She stared, eyes goggling. It wasn't possible!

Sukey pinched herself. Yes, she was still here, it wasn't a dream. She stared at the other girl and the other Sukey stared back.

Then the other girl, this almost mirror image, got out and came towards her, smoothing down her frothy pink dress, patting her pink hair ribbons and neat, shining hair.

Sukey wiped her grubby hands on her jeans and swallowed.

'Gosh. Golly!' she said nervously. 'Who are you?'

'Susanna! At last!' cried the other girl hugging and kissing her like a long-lost friend. 'It said you'd come. It said it would be tea time and It was right.'

'What It?' Sukey asked, wiping the kiss off.

'My friend, It. It's a sort of . . . Oh, I'll show you later, Susanna.'

'Everyone calls me Sukey at home.'

'Sukey. Of course. Well, Sukey, you

don't look very glad to see me!' said the
other girl. 'I thought you'd be *really
really* pleased.'

'Oh, I am, I am,' said Sukey. What
else could she say? 'So you were
expecting me, then?'

'Yes. Come inside.' The other girl
slipped past Sukey into the house.

'Wipe your feet,' she added as she stepped daintily inside.

Sukey went in.

'So, how does it feel to have one's dreams come true?' said the girl.

'What?' Sukey stood in the bright little room feeling big and dirty.

'You're nine today, aren't you? Didn't you see your card?'

'My card?'

'And you were, weren't you, just thinking how you'd like a sister? Perhaps gazing into the distance longingly? Imagining what she might look like?'

'A sis . . . ?' Sukey choked. 'I did, I think I did, yes, sort of mention a sister,' she admitted. 'Just to myself, just a thought . . .'

'Well, here I am!' she cried. 'Your twin sister.'

'Twin? Sister? . . . But it's not possible . . .' said Sukey.

But it *was* possible because this other girl, though not identical, was very like her, she had to admit.

Somehow she had masses of all the bits of Sukey that Sukey didn't have enough of. For a start she was really pretty. She was clean too and neat and tidy. She looked kind, even sensible and good. And she was so smooth! Smooth as plastic . . . Sindy! She's just like Sindy, thought Sukey. Blue-eyed and squeaky clean just like a plastic doll and not real at all.

'Can I sit down?' she gasped, sinking on to the bed.

The other girl winced ever so slightly as Sukey crumpled the neat bed and squashed one of her dolls.

'I can see it's a bit of a shock, but I am your sister. More than a sister, a twin – your other half.'

Sukey tried to laugh; it sounded like a dog with a cough.

'But I only *thought* about having a sister, and it was a little one, not a twin. Mum's having another baby and I've got twelve brothers already.'

'Having twelve brothers doesn't mean you can't have a twin sister,'

said the girl kindly. 'We were separated when we were tiny. It was a
spell, like they did on Sleeping
Beauty.'

'What?'

'Sleeping Beauty. Because our
parents didn't invite Fairy Finkle
Bottle to our christening party – you
know how offended people get – well,
this fairy put a spell on us. Separated
us by putting me out here and you
over there.'

'On two sides?'

'Yes. But now you've found me and
we can be united. Here, have some ice-
cream.'

Sukey couldn't speak, or eat. Her
brain was whirring in its attempt to
understand. A baby taken away by a
bad fairy? A *fairy*? In her mind was
a picture, clear as clear, of two babies,
creamy smooth cheeks, closed eyes
with eyelashes long on a curved cheek
. . . Were they dolls? Real babies? Was
it a dream or had she seen them?

The clink of the other girl's spoon

against the bowl brought Sukey back to the present again.

'It can't be true! What about my parents? Do they know you're here?' gasped Sukey.

'*Our* parents,' the girl corrected her. 'No. Well, they did at the time, of course, but the spell made them forget. They won't remember until we break the spell.'

'It's just like a fairy story.'

'It is a fairy story. Your very own one. You are the only one who can free me from this spell.'

'Me?'

'Only you, my dear sister, my twin sister, only you can help.' She clutched her hanky to her trembling lips and cried: 'I have no name! I have no name! I'm the only person in the whole world who hasn't got their very own name and, until we find it, I shall be stuck here for ever!'

4. More About The Sister

'But hang on a minute,' said Sukey. 'Why don't you just come back to the house with me now? We can see Dad and . . .'

The other girl groaned. 'I can't.'

'Why?'

'Go outside and look,' she said, pushing Sukey out through the door. 'Look!'

The Spanglers' house was not there.

'What have you done with it?' cried Sukey.

'Nothing. Remember, you couldn't see this house before, could you?' Sukey shook her head. 'And now you're here, on *this* side of the magic spell, you can't see *that* house. You've crossed over and we can't cross back until we've found my name.'

Sukey sat down heavily. 'You mean I'm stuck here? With you?'

'But isn't that nice? You want a sister, don't you?'

'Yes, yes, of course,' said Sukey, patting her arm.

Sukey stared at the floor. But it's not how I wanted it, she thought. I didn't want a clever sister. I didn't want one prettier than me or cleaner than me . . . I didn't want it like this.

'I'm so looking forward to coming home,' said the other girl. 'Those brothers must be so adorable! Oh, how I want a family of my own!'

Who'd want a family like mine? Sukey thought. Ralph never talks to me, Henry smells, Claude only ever writes poetry and little Maxi, ah, he's so sweet, he's already trying to say my name, and Larry, such a darling little mushroom nose. Elvis, always singing 'Oh, Susanna', and Rikki . . .

'Hey!'

Sukey jumped as the other girl prodded her. 'Hey, what's that moving under your jumper?'

'Oh, nothing, it's just Smelly.'

'How disgusting! You mean, it's so smelly it's moving?'

'No, no, the football jumper's new. I mean Smelly is his name. It's my rat.' Sukey pulled him out proudly. 'Billy gave him to me.'

Smelly sniffed at the other girl with interest; she was quite smelly in her own way.

'He likes you,' Sukey admitted rather sadly.

'Of course he does, I'm just the same as you . . . Well,' said the sister, 'I suppose we'd better get going. We only have today to find it and I've never gone name searching before. Oh, won't it be a wonderful birthday present for you!'

'What's that?' asked Sukey as she was hurried out of the house.

'This one! *Me!* Just what you've always wanted!'

5. The Journey Starts

The sister locked the cottage then pulled on some white gloves and got into the car.

'Come on!'

Sukey looked once more in the direction of her home. Nothing. Just trees and a rising hill with more trees. Had they missed her yet? They'd wonder where she was. They'd be so worried . . . or would they? Her father was so busy with all the brothers, the cooking and shopping and building extensions, and any minute her mother would have that new baby boy . . . would anyone even notice that she'd gone?

Well, Sukey thought, getting into

the car, it'll just serve them right if I get eaten by wolves or something, then they'll wish they took more notice!

'They'll definitely miss me at bedtime,' she said out loud.

'Of course. Close the door. Off we go!' said the other girl and she started the car and away they went.

Fancy being able to drive, thought Sukey, and having your own car. She stared enviously at her new sister.

The other girl was so like her and yet so different. It was fascinating – like looking in a wobbly mirror at the fair. What if we suddenly met Danny or Grant or any of the boys right now? she thought. Would they know which one I am? We've got different clothes on, but that could easily be changed. Is she really my sister? I wish I felt pleased. At least she's a girl, at least she wouldn't buy me a golf score book. She's not quite what I wanted, not perfect . . . or perhaps she is, *too* perfect? Not what I'd have chosen, but then who gets to choose their family?

'Thinking about home?'

'Sort of . . .' lied Sukey.

'It must be brilliant with all those boys around!'

'Oh, no, it's awful! They all play boyish things and fight and blow pea-shooters and ride bikes and mend my scooter and make me toys for Smelly and furniture for the doll's house and . . .'

Who? What? Are those my brothers? Sukey gulped. What dear, charming boys they sounded!

'They sound wonderful!' said the other girl. 'Oh, it's all going to be such fun.'

Is it? thought Sukey, gloomily. Oh, why did I ever wish for a sister?

Sukey stroked Smelly as he poked his head out of her jumper. He twitched his nose, sniffing the fresh scents; his whiskers and ears streamed backwards in the wind. He was having fun. Well, she can't take Smelly away, thought Sukey, but then I don't suppose she wants to.

'It's different here,' said Sukey, gazing at the round hills and the distant blue mountains. 'It's very beautiful, and warmer.'

'And more dangerous,' said the sister quietly. 'Don't forget that all the bad things are on this side of the spell – the witches and wizards and warty things. That bad fairy is probably watching us right now and may even try to stop us.'

'Do you really think so?' Sukey asked, looking round nervously. 'I can't even believe we are in a spell. Spellbound – it's got a new meaning for me now – I feel tangled up in it all.'

'Just think of me, stuck here for the last nine years with only It to talk to.'

'What is this It you keep talking about?'

'I quite forgot it,' said her sister. 'It's in the dashboard. Do get it out.'

Sukey opened the little cupboard in front of her and peered inside.

'There's just a sort of ball,' she said. 'Is that what you mean?'

'That's it. It said you'd be here today. It seems to know everything, and it's going to help us on our search with directions and things.'

Sukey picked up the ball. 'YAH!' she cried, and nearly dropped it again. 'What is it?'

It was soft and squidgey to touch, like lumpy dough. She rolled it around and found it had a large crack in it, like a mouth.

'How does it work? Does it speak?'

'Just squeeze it,' said the sister. 'At

41

least, that's what I do.' So Sukey
squeezed it, and a rough noise, a sort
of loud BLURGH noise, came out of it.

'It's disgusting!' said Sukey. 'It went
Blurgh! at me.'

'Do it again, more softly.'

This time, when Sukey squeezed it,
the ball said quite clearly: 'Blar blar
blar blimey!' as if it were out of breath,
then puffed up and said, 'Up the hill.
Shop. Ask at the shop. Blar.'

'Well,' said the sister. 'Let's do it.'

6. The Name Shop

They turned up the hill, driving now
between big rocks and thin trees until
they came to a large flat slab of stone
into which some letters had been
chiselled:

MISS TAKE'S
NAME
SHOP

'Gosh, look!' cried the sister. 'This is going to be easy! Well done, old ball!'

Sukey looked at the ball suspiciously. Even though she didn't squeeze it, it suddenly went 'Bla bla bla,' like a round chuckle.

'Let's be careful, though,' said Sukey. 'I mean, why should it be so easy?'

The sister had jumped out of the car and was heading for the door. 'Come on!'

Sukey got out more slowly. Is this it then? she wondered. We get a name and go home and I have a new sister, ready-made? Just like that? I can't believe it.

'It can't be just any old name,' the sister was saying. 'It has to be mine. My real one. Oh, do hurry.'

The name shop was actually a very large damp cave whose walls were lined with crooked, zigzaggy shelves containing hundreds of wooden drawers. Some of the drawers were open and Sukey could see millions of cards inside, each one printed with a name.

'Hello, dearies,' said a little voice.

The girls stepped forward. There, seated behind a vast desk was a tiny old woman. 'I'm Miss Take,' she said, smiling toothlessly. 'Looking for a name?'

'Yes,' said Sukey.

'I'm her sister,' said the sister, 'but I don't have a name.'

'A sister's name, eh,' muttered the old woman, looking from one girl to the other. 'You want your own, do you? Something special, I suppose?'

She pulled open a long drawer and leafed through some cards. 'Fancy any of these? Esmerelda? Edwina? Ernestine? Elizabeth?' She looked up at them, but the sister shook her head. 'No? No? Oh, very particular, aren't we? Got something special in mind?' She didn't wait for an answer, but slammed the drawer shut, dived across to the other side of the cave and flung open more drawers. Bits of paper, filing cards and pens went flying. 'Simona. Shelley. Sharon. Sindy. *Susanna . . .*'

'But that's my name!' cried Sukey. 'I mean, everyone calls me Sukey, but . . .'

'Be careful,' warned Miss Take. 'Use your name properly or you might lose it. I've some spare Susannas here. What about one for her? Just think how much easier it will be for everyone. One name tape for both school uniforms – you could share everything! And when your parents call you: SU-SANNA, SU-SANNA!' her shrill voice echoed horribly round the cave walls, 'you'll both go running . . .'

'No, no!' Sukey cried. 'No, I've changed my mind. We don't want your names at all.'

'I just want my name,' said the sister. 'I don't know what it is, but I'll recognize it . . .'

'I've got more under here,' said Miss Take, watching them carefully. She scuttled back to the desk again like a giant spider. 'Different ones.' She lowered her voice to a scratchy whisper, as she began opening the desk drawers. 'Ooh, these are lovely names: Meanie. Cross-patch. Fatty. Green-eye . . . for the jealous ones, you know.' She looked pointedly at Sukey.

Sukey looked away. What did she think? Pooh! Her, jealous? No way!

'Or I've got Stinky. Cowardy-custard. Po-face . . . do any suit?'

Sukey giggled.

'I just want my *real* name,' said the sister. 'Where can I go to get my *real* name?'

The old woman slammed the desk drawers shut, folded her arms and stared bad-temperedly at them. 'How dare you! These are real names, aren't they? I bet you haven't even any money to pay for one, anyway. Names don't come cheap. Names are expensive, take a lot of working out . . .'

'I think we'd better go . . .'

'Go? Not likely! Not just like that with no names given or bought or anything at all!' The tiny woman jumped up on to the chair and waved her fist angrily. 'You people are all the same,' she shouted, 'expecting something for nothing and it won't do, it won't do!'

'Sorry,' said Sukey. She turned and whispered to the other girl: 'It was that rotten blah ball! It got us into this.'

'You've no money I suppose?' said Miss Take, hopefully. The girls shook their heads. 'Thought so. Thought so. All right. Names. Names, now what have we got? Here's a riddle, get it right and I won't keep you or your names. Get it wrong, and into the drawers you go!'

Sukey shuddered. 'Go on, then.'

The little woman cackled with delight. 'You won't get it, you won't get it – not your name neither, silly little girlies . . .'

'We're waiting,' said Sukey.

'Right. Right. Well. There are two goldfish swimming in a bowl, round and round. How do you know that the one in front is called Bob?'

The sister rolled her eyes to the ceiling blankly . . . she had no idea.

Sukey smiled. There was one thing about her brothers, and that was they loved jokes and they told them all the time. This was one of their favourites.

'Don't know,' said the sister.

'Oh, I do,' said Sukey quickly. 'You

know it's Bob, because the one behind
will be swimming along going like
this . . .' and she opened her mouth
wide, like a fish, and said almost
silently: 'BOB, BOB, BOB,' letting
her lips plop together as if she were
blowing a bubble.

Sukey hooted with laughter, just as
she had when Jake had told her the
joke.

The old woman did not seem to find
it so funny.

She got down from her chair and
began slamming the long drawers
shut. 'Didn't want your names, anyway,' she said, 'especially not yours.'
She pointed at the sister.

'But I haven't got one.'

50

'That's what you think,' said Miss Take. 'That's all you know. Go on, you can go. Spoil-sports.'

They didn't need to be told twice and they hurried out into the daylight quickly before the old woman changed her mind.

Sukey stroked Smelly beneath her jumper. 'But I'm glad,' she whispered to him. 'I didn't really want her to get her name, I really didn't. I'm scared of taking her back home. I'm scared of having a real sister! I really am.'

Back in the car, the sister picked up the ball and squeezed it roughly.

'You rotten thing!' she shouted. 'My name wasn't there at all!'

'Blah BLAH BLARGH!' cried the ball in a choking voice.

'Now, please, where do we go now?'

'Blah bla up the hill, right up over the top blop.'

And the great mouth shut and refused to speak again.

'It's never been like this,' stammered the sister. 'This is a horrid side to it, horrid ball.'

'Better not squeeze it too hard,' said Sukey, 'or it might stop working.'

Then she saw that the sister was crying.

'I didn't mean to be unkind to it,' she sniffed. 'But it cheated us and I so want my name, you can't imagine how awful it is, how badly I want it! And we've only got today, only until the end of the day and then . . . we'll be stuck here for ever!'

'We'll do it, don't worry,' said Sukey.

'Perhaps I didn't understand the ball,' said the sister. 'Perhaps it meant *don't* stop at the shop or perhaps we stopped at the wrong one?'

'Maybe,' said Sukey, doubtfully. 'But I don't think we should trust it too much.'

They hadn't gone much further up the hill before they spotted a large plume of smoke rising up above the trees ahead, as if someone was having a bonfire.

'Let's go and see,' said the sister, steering towards it.

They bounced and wobbled over the uneven ground. 'I hope this doesn't damage the axle,' said the sister nervously. 'The suspension's not very good. We'll be sunk without the car.'

Axle? Suspension? And of course she can drive, too!

The rush of pity and kind feelings which had flooded Sukey only a moment ago now quickly drained away. Sukey felt jealous. Not only was this sister pretty and clean but she knew about axles and suspensions. The boys would adore her!

A shiver ran up her spine.

Suddenly the car jolted to a halt as the sister jammed on the brakes sharply.

'Look! What's that?' cried the sister pointing to a large wooden notice nailed to a tree.

'What odd writing,' said Sukey. 'What does it say? . . . There's a G and an A and an N, I think, and then B,I,G,B,O,T. Big bot? Is there a big bottom round here?' She giggled.

The sister didn't laugh.

'Look at the first letters: G,I,A,N,T.'

'G-ian-t, gi-ant, oh, GIANT!' cried Sukey. 'Giant! But it can't be a real one.'

'Why not? This is fairy tale land, remember? The other side, where the bad things are!'

Sukey shivered again. This place was certainly bringing out the bad side of her and she didn't like it.

'And the other word is Bigabotti, I can read it now,' went on the sister. 'Italian, I should think. Bigabotti,' she repeated with an Italian accent. 'Yes, that's it.'

'Let's go back,' said Sukey. 'It's a trap. Remember the blah ball said to go over the top of the hill . . .'

'But you don't trust the ball, remember? Oh, come on, let's have a look,' said the sister, driving on. 'Some giants spend their whole time capturing little girls like us and locking them up – just think of all the names he'll know!'

'Oh, great,' said Sukey. *Brilliant idea . . .*'

They drove on through the trees until a great cloud of smoke billowed around them, forcing them to stop. When the thick, choking fog had cleared they found themselves staring straight at . . . THE GIANT!

7. *Giant Bigabotti*

Giant Bigabotti was enormous; his head was the size of a garden shed, his legs and arms thicker than tree trunks. His fat fingers were like great bunches of white bananas.

Seeing the girls, he grinned a massive grin.

'Greetings, signorine,' he roared. 'Lucky day! Eet must be a dinner time? Yes?'

The sister nudged Sukey.

'No,' said Sukey.

The giant was looking at her as if she were the last cream bun in the baker's shop window. It made her feel queasy.

The giant looked at his watch, then at the fire. 'Eet is,' he said, 'eet really is and the water's a-hota, too.'

They all stared at the steaming pan hung over the fire. Inside, large, pale, knobbly-looking objects bubbled up and down.

'Eetsa stew,' explained Giant Bigabotti. 'But not lika ma mama used to maka me,' he added sadly.

'Well, I'm very sorry about that,' said the sister. 'But, actually, we are looking for my name and I just wondered if you could give us a clue or some advice . . . ?'

'Advice? Sure!' He bent towards them. 'RUN FOR IT!'

His smile exposed huge, brown, stumpy teeth, and an evil smell like stagnant pond water and rotting bones blasted the girls.

'Yikes! What a stink!' cried Sukey. 'Come on, let's get out of here!'

The sister revved up the car noisily, the wheels spun round – but the car didn't move. Sukey looked round

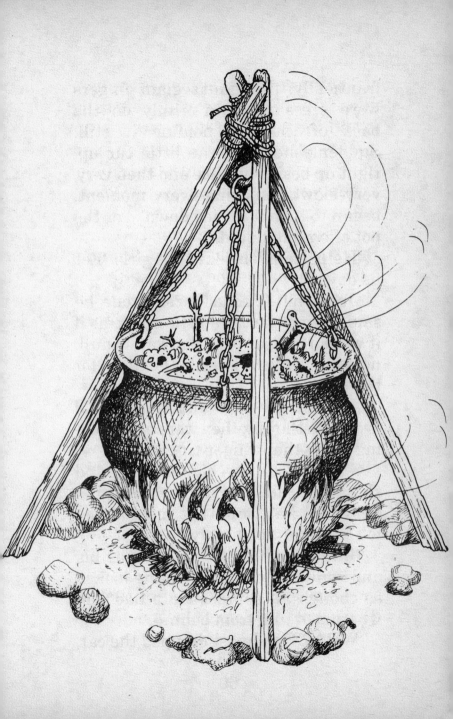

frantically: the giant's giant fingers were pressing down firmly on the back of the car, holding it still. Suddenly he lifted the little car up, right up beside his face and then very, very slowly, enjoying every moment, began to turn it upside down over the pot of boiling liquid.

'Help! Help!' shrieked the girls. 'Let us down!'

'Just what I needa for ze flavour,' he said, giving the car a little shake as if it were a pepper pot. 'Eet was so dull, nota much meat, I needa the flesh, for the taste!'

Any minute now and they would drop into the pot; they were only holding on by their finger-tips!

Sukey took a big breath and shouted the first thing she could think of: 'HEY! Fat Bum! Let me go!' She felt better immediately.

Giant Bigabotti's eyes grew as big and round as dustbin lids; he looked as though an express train had just whammed him from behind.

'WHA'?' He almost dropped the car,

but snatched at it again and then laid it upright on the ground. 'Whataya saying? My bum isa big?' He bit his lower lip and his eyes glistened damply. 'You saying thisa to me?'

'Far too big. You're fat. You've got bad breath. You're out of condition. You are a slob.'

Sukey's elder brothers prided themselves on their big muscles. They did sit-ups and press-ups and pull-ups; they raced each other round the assault course they'd made in the garden. She knew all about biceps and triceps and pectoral muscles, and the giant hadn't got any.

What she said was rude, but Ralph had said it to his father and it *had* made the giant put down the car.

'You're a-right. It'sa true,' said the giant sadly. 'My mama woulda said the same. Fatty. Porky. Bigabuma. Ah, what am I gonna do?' His enormous chest heaved with emotion and a large tear dribbled down through the stubble on his cheek.

What a dimbo, Sukey thought. She

got out of the car and went over to him.

'It's your diet,' she said quite kindly. 'Too much fat and too much . . . are those cow bones?'

'They are,' said Giant Bigabotti proudly. 'Lovely legs and hooves of the cow. And thatsa bit of rabbit and,' he poked around with his spoon, 'a bita horse, I think.'

'Foul!' said Sukey.

'Fowl? Sure, I gotta fowl too, some chicky and a pheasant, maybe two, I don'ta remember.'

'That's it! It's the meat. Haven't you heard of vegetarianism?'

'Vegitariwhati?'

'Vegetarianism. Means you don't kill furry animals (or little girls). You eat only green things. Much healthier,' said Sukey brightly. 'No big fat bum and live longer.'

'Ah, greena? Sometimes you leave the meat it goesa greena. OK?'

'No! No meat ever, at all. Instead, you eat celery and spring greens!

Mmm, buttered carrots . . .'

The sound of the car engine suddenly revving into life, stopped her in mid-flow. The sister was escaping on her own!

'Hey!' cried Sukey. 'Don't go.'

The giant put his hand back on to the car, quietly, firmly.

'Stop it,' he said. 'I'ma listening.'

'Er, um, and new potatoes spotted with fresh mint!' Sukey went on, nervously. 'Fresh ripe tomatoes. Parsnips and cucumber, lettuce and watercress. Delicious!' She tried to sound calm but there was a horrid panicky feeling in her tummy. Why had the sister started the engine? She wouldn't really leave her, would she?

'That soundsa good,' said the giant, 'but I'va no greens. See, justa the cows and the sheeps . . .'

'No greens?' cried Sukey, warming to her subject, 'no greens? Why, it's ALL green. Look! Grass, heather, ferns, bushes, trees, all healthy eating stuff. Try it. Try peeling it, cutting it and cooking it. Write a book about it, I bet it would be a great success. *The Natural Way To Eat Out.*'

The giant liked the idea of being famous and selling his book. It felt like the book was already written and he was going to be invited to go on telly. He grinned and grinned and grinned.

'Ah, vegitaryissi. It'sa good. I'ma gonna try it.'

'So pleased to have been of help,' said Sukey, edging backwards towards the car. 'You might do us a favour in return. We've got to find a name for my sister here. You don't know anything about names, do you?'

'Nah. I never give the dinner itsa name. Bad taste. Very bad taste. No good for the flavour. Now, I'm gonna go getta me some greenies. Goodabye.'

8. The Tricky Troll

'Well done,' said the sister, as they set off again. 'You were brilliant!'

'Not really!'

'You were! You saved us from the giant. Thank goodness I've got you!'

'I just did what I could . . .'

'But that's what sisters are for, aren't they?'

Sukey nodded. A warm glow filled her insides. She isn't bad, this funny sister, she thought, peeping at her sideways. I just wish she wasn't so clean and so, *just so*!

'You know, for one awful moment back there, I thought you were trying to escape when you started the engine,' she admitted.

'Oh, Sukey! How could you? As if I'd leave you! You're my sister, my other half and I need you. I don't know how you could think such a thing!'

Sukey blushed. She was right. How could she think it? I'm just jealous and horrid, she admitted, but I will try and be nice to her. I will.

'I'm sorry,' she said. 'I think it's this place. It makes me odd. Giants and

fairies and that ball. I've never talked to a ball before or a giant.'

'They're the only sort of things I ever talk to,' said the other girl. 'You can't imagine how awful it is. The witches are the worst, so sneaky and such liars.'

'And all because our parents didn't invite someone to our christening party?'

'Yes. It happens all the time. I bet the fairy wasn't just offended, I bet it was jealous, too. Twin girls! Can't you imagine how pleased everyone else must have been after all those boys!'

'Mmm. Shame neither of us was secretly a princess,' said Sukey, wistfully. 'That would have been fun, wouldn't it?'

'Now you're being silly,' said the sister. 'We're both very ordinary, except I haven't got a name. And that's what I need to break out of this spell and back into the other world. That's all.'

Just then, rounding a large rock,

they saw the river below. It was like a brilliant shining ribbon bending and snaking through the green valley. Their track led straight down the hill to an old rickety bridge across the water.

'Better ask the ball,' said the sister.

'But it just leads us into more trouble!'

'But what else can we do? Let's give it a chance. It was right about you coming and everything, wasn't it?' The sister gave the ball a gentle squeeze.

'Blah blurgh blidge. River. Cross water. By blidge.'

'Well, that's the way the path goes,' she said. She peered up at the sky. 'What time is it? We've only got until the sun goes down to break this spell.'

'Come on then, let's go for it,' agreed Sukey.

They drove down the winding path towards the river, the wind flying their hair back, the wheels scrunching on the gravel.

They slowed down as they approached the bridge.

'Do you think it's strong enough to take the car?' said Sukey.

'I don't know. It's the only way over . . .'

Suddenly there was a loud squelching noise, like a wellington boot being yanked out of mud and a great toad-like creature jumped out beside them, splattering water all over the place.

'Aaagh!' they screamed.

Standing right in front of them was a big green troll.

Sukey stared at him in horror and disgust. He was revolting. He was covered in slime which seemed to ooze out of his lumpy, warty skin and his mouth was huge and slobbery with sharp teeth. Tufts of wiry hair sprouted from the largest lumps on his head, back and hands. His feet were webbed and both his hands and toes had long dirty claws.

'Oh, no! That rotten ball's landed us in it again!'

'Hoy, you!' cried the troll. 'Shtop! Go no further! Shtop!'

He had such a lot of slime in his mouth it came out in a spray and made his words all blurred and squidgey.

'Thish is my bwidge! You must pay a toll to this twoll if you want to pash.'

'A toll? What's that?'

'Hoy! You know, no cheating! A fee. A penalty.'

'We don't have any money,' said Sukey. 'What will happen if we don't pay?'

'I'll eat you, shkinny little shticks as you are.'

'Perhaps you know Giant Bigabotti? He lives up that hill,' said Sukey, bravely. 'He didn't bother with us, he's become a vegetarian. Do you want to know about the green . . .'

'Boiled bwoccoli, yarh!' The troll spat; blobs of yellow and green showered the car. 'Meaty bones, gwistle and gwavy, that's what I like. Don't give me baked beans when I can

have baked bwains! Shteak and shausages, not shwede and shelery!'

The girls shuddered.

'Do you think we really have to go over this bridge?' whispered Sukey. 'Perhaps if we . . .'

'Oh, thish is the way,' grinned the troll. 'The only way. See?' He pointed to a notice: NUMEROUS NAMES it said, and the arrow pointed across the river to the other side. 'Thish is defnish . . . definesh . . . duffnesh . . . the way.'

'All right,' said Sukey. 'What's the toll? We haven't any money, though, and we must cross the bridge.'

The troll chuckled. 'Hee, hee, that's it! Thash it! The toll. Not money, no. Ho, ho, girlish for lunch and girlish for tea, girlish on toast and all just for me!'

The girls shivered in disgust.

'Just tell us what you want,' pleaded Sukey.

'Come,' he said, waddling forward.

Warily, they got out of the car.

The troll pointed to the bridge roof where a sharp blade, like that in a guillotine, was suspended. Below, placed directly under the blade, was a small wooden table.

'Heesh, sheesh, sheesh,' he chortled, trembling like an old, mouldy blancmange. He looked from the girls to the blade. 'Watch!' he cried and, suddenly, with a steely 'WHOOSH!' the silver blade shot down on to the table with a thud, sending splinters of wood flying.

'Ha, ha, heesh, heesh,' cried the troll, hobbling and wobbling from one webbed foot to the other. 'Cutsh off anything. Sharper than a razor. Cutsh through bone: fingersh and legsh, hee, hee. Cutsh you off jusht wight for me!'

The troll began to wind the blade back up into its place in the roof of the bridge.

'Is that it?' asked Sukey. 'What are we supposed to . . . ?'

'Now,' said the troll, 'your toll. I call this, *Beat The Blade!*'

He held up a small green pea to show them, then he placed it right in the centre of the table, exactly where the blade had carved a deep groove from its many cuts. Then he stepped backwards again.

'Er . . .' Sukey couldn't speak. She took a big breath and tried again. 'Er, b-b-beat it?'

'Yesh. Beat it, yesh! Move the pea before the blade comesh down – THWACK! Ha, ha, heesh, heesh! It's Beat The Blade time!'

9. Carrots

Sukey thought, I never really wanted a sister anyway. If I make a run for it now . . . She glanced at the other girl and saw, saw as though they were written there, the same thoughts going through her head. Their eyes met and for a moment it was like looking straight into a mirror. I can't, thought Sukey. She's part of me. I'm part of her. I can't go.

The sister grinned, the moment was broken.

'Easy!' she said.

She walked over to the table and looked up at the blade, then down at the table again and the little pea sitting right in the middle of it. Then she bent down, chin level with the table top, knees bent, arms poised.

'Weddy?' gasped the troll, trembling with excitement.

'Quite!'

The troll put his hand on the lever: 'NOW!' and he let go of the rope.

Down shot the blade with a terrible sharp sound and glint of steel. Sukey winced; she'll never do it, she thought, I'm going to faint when there's all that blood . . .

But as soon as the blade began to move, the sister opened her mouth and blew . . . HARD!

And the green pea rolled across the table and the blade thundered down into nothing but wood. There was no awful sound of bones smashing or blood spurting, and Sukey breathed again.

'Aow! Aow!' cried the troll, throwing his arms up in the air. 'No. No. No. NO!' He stamped on the pea with his flipper-like feet, slime flying. 'You cheatsh! CHEATSH!'

'Gosh, well done!' said Sukey. 'Really clever. I would never have thought of blowing it away, never in a million years.'

The sister grinned happily. 'Thanks,' she said.

So we've saved each other, Sukey thought. It's really odd how there are certain things she can do and certain things I can do. We're like two halves that work like one together. I think I've been missing her all my life. She smiled warmly at the other girl.

But the troll was not happy.

'It was cheating!' the troll repeated. 'It'sh not fair. Miserable pea . . . Trusht a veg to let me down. I won't let you thwew, I won't!'

'What? What did you say? Vegetables?' Sukey suddenly thought of something. 'Look here,' she said to the troll, 'since you so enjoy games, I know a good one . . . Claude did this to all of us and it always works,' she whispered to the other girl. 'But if you can't do it,' she told the troll, 'you've got to let us go over the bridge.'

'What game? What twick?' asked the troll, suspiciously.

'I bet,' said Sukey, 'that I can read your mind.'

'Never,' said the troll, shaking his head, 'never.'

'All right, we'll see,' said Sukey. Quickly she wrote the word CARROT on a scrap of paper and handed it to her sister for safe-keeping.

'Ready?' she asked. The troll nodded. 'OK, close your eyes . . .'

'I will not!' spluttered the troll. 'You'll wun off, I know.'

'OK, OK, don't close your eyes, then, but concentrate, otherwise you won't have a chance. Ready?' The troll nodded. 'Right, think of a number less than ten . . . Double it,' Sukey went on, 'add four, take away six, multiply by three . . .'

'Not so fasht! Not so fasht!' squealed the troll, screwing his eyes up in concentration.

'Have you multiplied by three?'
'Yesh.'
'Add seven, double it, then take

79

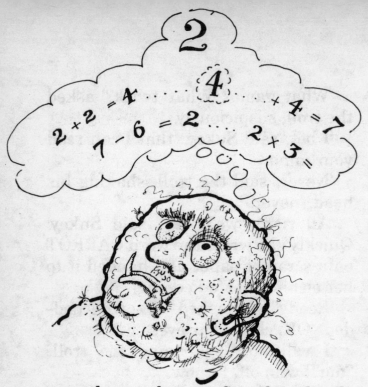

away the number you first thought of.'

The troll nodded, nodded again, then grinned smugly.

'Got it, got it,' he smirked.

'Now, quickly,' Sukey instructed, 'what's the first vegetable you can think of?'

The troll peered at her, thoughts flickering almost visibly across his green face. He looked in pain, he looked apologetic, he opened his mouth and said:

'Carrot?'

'Ha, ha!' cried Sukey, thrusting the paper into his face. 'You said it, you said it! I knew you would!'

'But, but,' stammered the troll, looking at the word CARROT with horror. 'What about all thoshe numbersh?'

'Just to confuse.'

'Howid. Hateful!' He sank down into a sort of dollop of green beside the bridge, muttering and spluttering. 'It'sh not fair!'

Quickly, the two girls got back into the car and drove over the bridge. Smelly and Sukey watched behind but the troll didn't try and follow.

'How did you know he'd say carrot?' asked the sister.

'There's nothing to it,' Sukey admitted. 'I don't know why, but everyone always says carrot. They did when Claude did it to us anyway.'

'Everyone? Always?'

'Yes.'

'Pooh! I bet I wouldn't.'

10. The Magic Gate

Once they were safely on the other side of the river, the sister got out the ball and squeezed it crossly.

'You're supposed to help us!' she shouted. 'But all you do is lead us into trouble!'

The ball's mouth gaped open but it didn't speak.

'Never mind,' said Sukey. 'I never thought much of your blah ball.'

'No, but it was all I had,' the sister reminded her. 'And it lied.'

'The notice on the bridge pointed to names this way,' said Sukey, 'and there's only one way to go, so come on.'

'All right,' sniffed the sister quietly.

Smelly poked his nose out and

Sukey gave him some biscuit crumbs from her pocket. She was thinking about everyone at home.

They must be missing her by now. Had Mum had the baby? Was he all right? Please, please let the baby be all right, she willed. If only they could find this missing name and get back home.

'It's getting late,' said the sister suddenly.

Sukey looked around. Yes, the light was beginning to fade. The shadows were longer. I wonder what time it is, she thought. She could picture her brothers having a wonderful time at home, playing pass the parcel and musical chairs. Why did I think such bad things of them, she wondered. They're wonderful, and without them – their jokes and games, I'd never have even got this far.

'Don't worry, we'll find your name soon,' Sukey promised.

The sister smiled. 'Thanks. You know, I *knew* it would be like this. I'm so glad I found you. There's nothing quite like a sister, is there?'

'Nothing,' agreed Sukey with a smile.

Soon they came to a high wall which seemed to stretch for miles along the road. At last they came to some iron gates and they stopped the car and got out.

While their backs were turned an odd thing happened. The glove compartment opened and out rolled the blah ball. It plopped down on to the floor, rolled quietly out of the car and across the path where it disappeared in the long grass beside some boxes. Neither of the girls noticed a thing.

The boxes beside the gate were full of fruit: apples, pears, plums and cherries. The air was thick with their sweet, sickly smell.

Peering in through the iron gates, the sisters could see rows and rows of rich colourful trees stretching out into the distance.

'Good afternoon, ladies,' said a voice suddenly.

They spun round. Sitting beside the fruit boxes was a thin old man.

'Gosh, where did he spring from?'

'He wasn't there before, was he?' asked the sister.

'Er, hello,' said Sukey. 'Do you know anything about names . . . ?'

'Bla, not me,' grunted the man from under his hat.

'Oh.' The two girls looked at each other. There was something familiar about his voice. They peered at him, but he kept his face hidden beneath his hat.

'I don't think he'll be much help,' whispered the sister.

Sukey stared through the gates at the trees again – then she looked harder and longer.

'Oh, look!' she cried.

'Just fruit trees,' said the sister, peering through the iron bars.

'No, look, some of them have labels hanging off, look, over there and there!'

The old man shuffled and coughed. From beneath his hat, he said: 'Labels have names on them. A label is a name.'

'You said you didn't know about names!' cried the sister.

The old man laughed. 'I'm a friend of the troll. We both tell lies.'

'Nothing is ever what it seems in this place,' said Sukey. 'You shouldn't tell lies, you know. Are you sure we haven't met before?' she added, trying to peep under the man's hat.

'Blah no.'

'What?'

'Oh, leave him, Sukey. Let's try and get in this place and look at the labels. Do you think we can go in?'

'Of course you can,' said the man.

They pushed but the gate didn't move. There was no handle or latch.

'We can't get in!' said Sukey.

'Certainly you can get in, if you can open the gate.'

'I see,' said the sister. 'I thought there'd be a catch somewhere.'

'Bla of course there's a catch. Don't all gates have catches?'

'Ooh, I hate this sort of thing,' said the sister. 'Why must there be a catch? I just want my name. Just my name!'

Keeping his face hidden, the old man came over to them on small, quiet feet. 'Look carefully. On this side there is an iron gate but behind it is a wooden gate. To enter this magical orchard of names and labels you must push the wooden gate *through* the iron gate.'

'How do you mean? Open them back to front?' said the sister. 'Impossible! How can we get that great thing through there?'

The old man smiled. 'You must find out soon,' he said mildly, 'or it will be too late . . .'

'Too late?' cried Sukey. 'Don't say

that. It's ages till sunset, ages and ages . . .'

She stopped. The old man was taking off his hat. Masses of long white hair fell down about his face and down to his knees. He lifted his face up to hers. He had blue twinkling eyes and a massive wide mouth that spread from ear to ear.

'You! It's the blah ball! I thought I recognized your voice!'

The man slipped his arms from the rough jacket and silently shook himself. He had two small silvery wings on his back.

'Yikes! What are you?' cried Sukey.

'Fairy Finkle Bottle,' said the old man. 'Surely you remember? And also, as you guessed, your travelling companion, the blah ball.'

'Oh, no!' cried the sister.

'Oh, yes, and in a little while your time for name hunting will have run out and Sukey and you will stay here on the other side of the spell for ever and ever and ever . . .'

'I won't! I can't!' cried the sister. 'Why did you cheat us? Why make us go to all those horrid people and nearly get eaten and captured and everything?'

'Games,' said the fairy. 'I love them.' He chortled softly, stroking his shimmering wings. 'And you did very well, better than I expected. Perhaps you really do want a sister, Sukey.'

'Of course I do and there's still a chance, isn't there?' said Sukey. 'I know there is or we wouldn't be here now and you wouldn't be talking to us. Tell us about the gate again, tell us!'

'I'm nothing without a name,' said the sister sadly. 'Everyone must have a name. Other children don't have all this trouble; their parents just pick a name out of a book.'

'And you must pick yours out of a tree,' said the fairy. He picked up a peach and bit it. 'To get your name you must find the tree. To reach the tree you must open the gate. To open the gate you must push the wooden gate through the iron gate.'

'All right! All right!' She was staring hard at the gates. 'But I don't understand!'

'We beat the troll and the giant,' said Sukey. 'We shan't let you get us. No way!' She stared at the fairy. 'Why on earth do you want us here, anyway?'

'Ask yourself why you wanted a sister?'

'Because, because . . . Because I haven't got one,' said Sukey.

'And I haven't got one of *you* . . . YET!'

'Oh!' Sukey stepped back. 'Come on, sister! We've got to open the gate and find your name! We can do it together!'

The sister climbed up and began pulling and tugging at the wooden gate beyond. 'I bet it collapses,' she said, pulling at it. 'Or there's a hidden spring and it all folds up so you can slot it through the bars . . . There must be a secret button . . .'

'What did he say again?' Sukey muttered. 'Push the wooden gate through the iron one . . . But he might be lying again . . . who knows?'

'Even here there are rules,' said the fairy. 'I have to keep to them, we all do. I can't just capture you, nor could the troll or Giant Bigabotti, not unless you fail the tests. I let you get so far . . . and you've got further than I thought, but now . . . now it looks as though you'll be staying here for a long, long time.'

Sukey looked from the fairy to the gate and back again. Each time he had used exactly the same words; the answer was in the pattern of the words. She tried to make them into a picture, to read the words differently.

'I've got it!' she cried. '"Push it through" doesn't mean what it sounds like. It just means you have to push one gate while your hand is through the other gate . . .'

'Go on, do it then!' cried the sister.

Cautiously, Sukey fitted her hand through the bars of the iron gate so she touched the wooden gate behind, and pushed gently. At the tiniest pressure, the wooden gate swung open and, seconds later, so did the iron one.

11. Numerous Names

'Not blahd,' said the fairy. His eyes did not twinkle any more. 'Now, slowly, take it slowly, find her name!'

'Don't take any notice of him,' said Sukey. 'Quick, we need to be quick.'

The orchard was green and rich and luscious, and it smelt of newly-mown grass and soft, sugary fruits. The trees seemed to crowd round them, squeezing out the air with their whispering leaves. The swaying fruit, bobbing as if on a sea, oozed out a sweet, fruity stickiness.

Sukey yawned. It was like being trapped inside a bottle of sweets on a hot day.

The fruit smells woke Smelly and

he crept out from under Sukey's shirt to investigate. He thought the orchard was a lovely place and bounded away sniffing and nibbling at the fallen fruit.

Sukey had been about to fall asleep but Smelly's sharp claws scratching her skin woke her up again.

'It's a dangerous sort of place,' warned Sukey, trying not to yawn. 'Don't close your eyes! Try and keep awake. Keep moving. The name must be on one of the labels.'

They began searching the trees and, although the labels did have names on them, they weren't quite the right sort of names.

For example, on the cherry tree there were the following labels: RED, RIPE, GLACÉ, KIRSCH, MORELLO. And on one apple tree, Sukey read: GREEN, RED, SOUR, SWEET, while on another, she read: RIPE, HARD, CALVADOS, OF ONE'S EYE, PIE, CHUTNEY.

'Labels, like I said,' said the fairy quietly, coming up behind Sukey.

'I know. Mummy has Kirsch at Christmas. It's made from cherries.'

The fairy was so close, Sukey could feel his hot breath on the back of her neck. She moved away, but he followed, never letting her out of his sight.

The other sister was still reading the labels, running from one tree to the next. 'They're all silly! They're not real ones! It's not fair!'

'You don't think your name could be Cherry or Conference, like the pear?' asked Sukey hopefully.

'No, it could not!'

'Sorry.'

'We must look everywhere! On every single tree. In the branches, on the trunk, go on! My name is here somewhere. I know it is!'

Sukey wandered off amongst the trees, letting the scent waft over her. The smells of the ripe fruit were so sweet and rich, she could hardly breathe . . . So what if they didn't find the name? Who cared anyway? She just felt like lying down in the long grass and going to sleep.

The fairy, never far behind her, always watching her, chuckled quietly, and just as Sukey finally gave in and sat down, he flicked his fingers, dancing his fingertips until tiny sparkles scattered through the air . . .

'Ah-ha!' cried the sister suddenly and Sukey turned round, just missing the silvery sleeping spell as it flew through the air towards her.

'Look! Look!' She was pointing to the trunk of an old, gnarled apple tree where there was a tiny door with a brass handle and keyhole.

'A key! We have to find the key!'
cried the sister. 'My name is inside
that tree, I know it is. Oh, any
moment now, any moment now . . .
Don't stand there dreaming, please,
dear, dear sister, go and look for it! It's
getting darker, oh, I'm sure the sun's
going down, come on, come on!'

'It's too late, too late,' said the soft,
sweet voice of the old man. 'Take your
time. No hurry now.'

'No! Don't listen to him. Get looking! If only we had more time, or more clues. The key could be anywhere.'

They stared at the little door.

'It's a very odd keyhole,' said the sister.

'It's in a very odd place for a keyhole,' said Sukey. 'And it's a big keyhole for such a small door, and look at the edges, all uneven . . . it reminds me of something . . .'

Smelly, having eaten his fill, came back and began climbing up Sukey's leg on his way to his bed under her shirt.

Sukey pushed him away. 'You're all yukky and wet!' she scolded. 'Take that apple core away. Drop it, Smelly, I'm not having that under my . . .'

'STOP!'

The sister's voice was so loud that three nearby cherries fell to the ground, as did Smelly and his apple core.

'What's the matter?'

'STOP! Wait!' cried the sister. 'Get that apple core!'

She dived on to the ground and grabbed it. 'It's the key! Look, it's the key!'

'The key? You can't open a door with an apple core . . .' But why not? she thought, anything can happen here. Oh, Smelly, dear Smelly, what a clever little rat you are!

Quickly, the sister fitted the core in the lock, a spring was released with a twanging sound and the bark door opened. Inside was a box. She took the box out. It was a small metal box, and fastened around it were two bands of brass which were held firmly closed by tiny brass nuts and bolts.

There was a label attached to it. THE MISSING NAME it said.

The Missing Name

12. Going Home

The fairy laughed nastily.

'But it's blaalocked. It's locked with nails and bolts and glue and screws and nuts. And *you* can't open it! You can't get your name out . . . It's getting dark, look how dark it is, you'll never make it, never, never . . .'

'We will. Stop it!' cried the sister.

'Our brothers!' cried Sukey. 'They'll be able to do it. They can do anything!' She'd called them *our* brothers! And she didn't even mind. 'Let's get back as fast as we can!'

Fairy Finkle Bottle sat down heavily in the grass.

'Blah,' he said. 'Blad luck! I thought I'd got you then. But you've still got to get to the other side. Still got to open the box. You'll never make it. Once over on this side, the spell holds tight!'

'We will!' cried Sukey.

They jumped into the car and sped away down the road, away from the orchard and the fairy, towards home.

The sky was growing darker by the minute, but the yellow rim of the sun was still lighting up the far edge of the sky as the car arrived back at the miniature house where the sister lived. Out they jumped and together they rushed across the lawn to where the Spanglers' house should have been, although they couldn't see it.

They'd got halfway across the grass when suddenly the sister, who was in front, bounced backwards as if she'd hit a massive invisible spring.

She tumbled on to the grass.

'What happened? What was it?' asked Sukey, helping her up.

'I forgot,' said the sister. 'I still don't have my name so I'm still stuck on this side of the spell!'

'The spell? Is it here then?'

Sukey edged forward. In two steps she came up against an invisible wall. She felt it gingerly. It was soft beneath her fingers and when she pushed, her fingers went right through, as if she were pushing against the skin of a massive stretchy soap bubble. It closed around her wrist and her hand vanished; her hand was on the other side.

'I didn't feel it before when I came

into the spell,' said Sukey. Then she remembered how crossing the lawn at four o'clock – how long ago it seemed now – there'd been a moment of coldness and a feeling of change and she'd nearly turned back. 'I did feel it!' she cried, 'but I came straight through. I could see your house!'

'It's not fair!' cried the sister. 'Now you can get through again, but I can't! And oh, Sukey, I feel so funny.'

Sukey looked at her carefully.

'You do look peculiar,' she admitted, taking her hand. 'You've lost your shine. You used to shine and look so clean and neat. Please, please try again, you *must* come in.'

'I can't. I know I can't.'

'Come on!' Sukey forced her on to her feet and up against the invisible wall, but the sister couldn't push through.

'I shall just have to go back and get this box open myself,' said Sukey. 'It won't matter. The moment it's open the spell will break.'

'Is that what you want, really?' asked the other girl.

'What do you mean? Of course it is . . . now. I know I wasn't sure before, but I am now. It's hard to say this, I don't want to sound soppy, but you belong with us. I know you do.'

'Thank you . . . Go on, then,' said the sister. 'It's all up to you.'

Sukey took the box and pushed at the magic wall. It reminded her of clingfilm but it was softer and she pushed her way through gently, cautiously, first a leg, then a shoulder, then one arm. For a moment she was poised, half in one world, half in the other . . .

'Goodbye,' she called, pressing forward . . . but something stuck.

'I can't do it! Something's sticking.'

It was the magic box. It would not come through.

Sukey slipped back through the wall into the enchanted world again. 'What shall I do?' she began, 'the box . . .' But then she stopped, amazed,

106

for in the past two seconds things on this side of the spell had altered. It had darkened, as though someone had washed the sky and trees and grass with purple.

Night was drawing very close.

Her sister had changed too. She was paler, a shadowy, dim figure dulled with the dusky purple.

'Sister, sister, dear!' cried Sukey. 'Are you all right? Hold on, please hold on. Look, here's the box,' she said, pressing it into her hands. 'It's got to stay here.'

'Well, it is mine,' said the sister in a small voice.

''Course it is. Hold on to it. I shan't be long. I'll get our brothers. They're boys, it's their sort of thing, they'll open it!'

'I wish . . . I wish I could just see them,' whispered the sister weakly. 'I did so want to . . .'

'You will!'

Sukey glanced round anxiously. It was so dark. Had the sun actually gone down? Was it too late? No, no, it couldn't be!

She ran at the invisible wall and burst through, blinking in the sunlight on the other side.

There was her dear house! At last! She looked back quickly. Nothing. It was as if none of the land on the other side of the spell existed. And here it

well, it is mine

was so light. As if time had been standing still, thought Sukey. As if there, we were in another, faster, sort of time where night was coming sooner.

She began to run.

13. Opening The Box

She had to hurry. Was there time to get the boys? She only needed a hammer or a chisel or a spanner . . .

A SPANNER!

A tiny spanner! A miniature adjustable spanner – just like the one Danny had given her this morning.

'That's what I want!' she yelled, racing up the stairs to her bedroom.

'Where did I put it?' she cried, tumbling Smelly back into his nest of straw, and beginning to search.

I know I put it down in here, I know I did, she told herself.

She pulled the covers off the bed, she searched her dolls' house, she looked in her treasure box. Everywhere. Tears welled up in her eyes. I'll never find it, she thought. I haven't got enough time. No time, no time. And my new sister, I'll lose her again . . . It must be dark out there. I'll be too late.

She paused. What had Danny said about it?

'It may not be just exactly what you want this minute,' he'd said, 'but the minute *will* come when it's exactly what you want.'

How right he was.

If only I'd known the right minute for it was coming so soon, she thought.

Where was it?

And Danny had said: 'Sorry it's not new, but you see it's very special, that's why it's been used a lot.'

She remembered turning the rather battered spanner round in her fingers. It was adjustable, although the working bits looked a bit rusty and she'd thought, what a useless object! How wrong she had been! And then she'd forgotten it, and put it down . . . but where?

Where was it?

Suddenly she saw it, lying on the windowsill beside the empty packet of Smarties. She paused, remembering seeing the roof of that little house . . . what a long time ago it seemed now . . . then she grabbed the spanner and ran helter-skelter down the stairs and back into the garden.

She sped across the lawn, expecting any moment to burst through into the other side of the spell, but it never came. Surely it hadn't gone? Was she too late?

Everything looked so normal.

Gingerly she inched forward, arms outstretched and suddenly there it was, the invisible barrier, but this time . . . *Sukey* couldn't get through!

'Sister! Sister!' she cried, pounding soundlessly on the wall. 'Are you there?' Her fists pushed against the stretchy membrane, but wouldn't go through. 'Are you there?'

As though from a long, long way away, there came a soft voice:

'Yes, I'm here. Help me!'

'I can't get through!' cried Sukey. 'But I've got the spanner. I know this will work. Danny said it would. He knew it would. Here it is!'

She pushed the spanner at the wall; for a moment it jammed, and then for an instant she knew her sister's hand touched it, held it, and it slotted through and disappeared on the other side.

'Thank you!' The voice floated back ghostly and thin. 'Oh, Sukey, it's very dark in here. Thank you for wanting me.'

'Hurry, hurry,' urged Sukey.

Any minute now and the sister would get that box open and get her name and leap through the wall out of the spell and into the Spanglers' world where she belonged.

'COME ON!' she yelled. She tried to picture her sister fumbling with the box, adjusting the spanner, fitting it on to the tiny brass bolts . . . come on, come on . . .

Suddenly a man's voice called:

'Sukey! Sukey!'

Sukey spun round, amazed to see her father there.

'Dad!'

'There you are! The boys said you'd gone to the loo but I thought you'd be out here.'

'Oh, Dad! It's you!'

'Of course it's me. Are you all right? What are you doing standing out here?'

'Have I been ages and ages?'

Her father glanced at his watch. 'About five minutes, darling,' he said. 'It's only just gone four . . .'

'It couldn't be! I've been gone ages and ages . . .'

'It doesn't matter, sweetheart. Listen, you missed the news!' he cried, swinging Max from one arm to the other. 'You missed the news! The baby's been born . . .'

'What?' She clutched at her father's hand. 'Born? Is he all right? Is Mummy all right?'

'Yes, yes. And guess what? No, you'll never imagine, it's too extraordinary and on your birthday too . . .'

Suddenly, Billy and Jake came rushing out of the house followed by Danny and Larry and Grant . . .

'It's a GIRL!' they yelled. 'It's a girl!'

14. The Last Chapter

Sukey couldn't speak. She could feel a smile stretching her face and she couldn't unstretch it enough to say a single thing.

'When you've got over your shock,' said her father, 'you must get thinking about a name. Mum says you can choose, Sukey.'

'Me? Me to choose?'

More names?

A baby sister and she could name it.

A twin sister with no name . . .

The twin sister! Sukey swung round reaching out desperately for the wall.

There was nothing there.

117

She moved forward cautiously . . . nothing. She walked on, hoping and hoping that the barrier would suddenly bang against her, but there was nothing at all. It had gone.

It had all gone.

A terrible sadness filled her. I was too late. I failed her. I failed my sister.

She turned away to cry. Tears pricked at her eyes, making the garden all sparkly and blurred so that for a moment Sukey was looking at something shining on the lawn, something glistening and silver, but not really believing it was there. Then she realized that it was her spanner. Her precious birthday spanner. And something else beside it, a small silver locket.

Sukey picked them up carefully. She stroked the locket, turning it over and over in her hand. The word GEMINI was inscribed in the silver on one side. Twins. She knew it meant that, because it was her birth sign. On the other was the word SPANGLER.

'What's that?' asked Billy, coming up.

'It's a locket.'

'What's inside?'

'I don't know.'

'Well, open it,' said Billy.

Sukey knew there would be a name inside. She knew there would be the name of a sister inside. And she couldn't help hoping, as she eased the sides apart, that the name wouldn't be quite as nice as her own. Perhaps Nora or Mildred, no, no, that would be too mean . . . She took a deep breath and read:

'Amelia.'

'What was that?' asked her father abruptly.

'AMELIA!' shouted some of the boys. 'Keep your hair on, Dad. It's just Sukey's name.'

'Not my name, but the one for the baby,' said Sukey.

On each side of the locket was a photograph of a baby. They looked like dolls, round waxy faces and long dark

lashes. Below each was a name: Susanna and Amelia.

'Fancy you choosing that name!' cried Mr Spangler. 'Extraordinary! It's made me feel quite sad, it really has.'

'Why?'

'Well ... well, oh ... What made you choose it? Such a coincidence!'

'It's written here,' said Sukey showing the locket to her father.

'Where did this come from?' he asked.

'I found it.'

'But it's your mother's. It's been missing ever since . . . well, oh, we never wanted to tell you. Fancy it turning up now. Nine years on . . .'

'Nine years ago? I see,' said Sukey, quietly. 'I think I understand. Don't be sad,' she added. 'It was a long time ago and now we've got another baby. And she's fine and she's a sort of twin, isn't she, seeing as this is my birthday.'

'You know, then?' Mr Spangler asked weakly.

'I think so. Everything's all right now.'

Sukey gazed across the lawn to where the tiny pink car and tiny little house had been and there was nothing. She knew her other sister had gone for ever but she had a real one now. Together they had found the baby's name and now the baby could come home.

Everything was all right.

Even the name was right, because Amelia was quite a nice name but not too fantastic and it would only be a little time before someone called her Melly and that would soon become

Smelly and that would keep her in her
place. Yes. Just like dear Smelly the
rat.

THE END

SHRUBBERY SKULDUGGERY
Rebecca Lisle

Sent to stay with unknown relatives while her
parents are abroad, Polly is delighted to discover
that 'The Shrubbery' turns out to be the most
wonderful house, with an even more wonderful
garden.

It's no surprise to Polly that such an enormous
garden, full of rare and beautiful plants, needs a full-
time gardener to look after it. But Miss Gargoyle
doesn't look - or act - like a real gardener at all.
And what on earth can have happened to Polly's
two uncles, who have been missing for days? With
the help of her cousin Harry, Polly sets out to keep
a close eye on Miss Gargoyle and soon discovers
that something very sinister indeed is going on in
the Shrubbery garden!

0 440 862779

THE WEATHERSTONE ELEVEN
Rebecca Lisle

'Ye eleven magical dogs of old
As once for Merlin, now find me GOLD . . .'

When ten ancient stone dogs are dug up at
crumbling old Weatherstone Hall in Cornwall,
Bella's archaeologist father is certain that they once
belonged to the great wizard Merlin. He whisks
Bella off with him to investigate immediately.

But only ten dogs have been found. Where is the
eleventh? As Bella sets out to find it, she becomes
strangely entangled in the history of the beautiful,
golden-haired hounds – and in a nightmare struggle
against mysterious forces. For the legendary magical
powers of the dogs have attracted the attention of
someone else – someone with some very 'fishy'
habits and a horribly sinister plan . . .

A FEDERATION OF CHILDREN'S BOOK
GROUPS PICK OF THE YEAR

0 440 863252

THE GENIE OF THE LAMPPOST
Rachel Dixon

'What is your command, Master?'

Everything's going wrong for Daniel. Bullied by a
rich new boy in town, he's been forced out of 'The
Mob' – the best gang around. Suddenly no-one
wants to know him any more. But then a very
unusual genie fizzles out of an old lamppost. Will
this mysterious visitor solve all Daniel's problems –
or land him in even deeper trouble?

'Entertaining and brightly written'
THE SCHOOL LIBRARIAN

0 440 863147

A SELECTED LIST OF TITLES
AVAILABLE FROM YEARLING BOOKS